J

THE WIZARD OF
WASHINGTON SQUARE

"I'm the Wizard of Washington Square."

From behind the door, into the sunlight, stepped the weirdest little man David had ever seen. He had a long, silky white beard that was parted slightly off center and flowed down to his waist. He was no taller than a four-year-old. He wore a robe of inky blue and a pointed hat that sparkled with stars.

"How do you do," said the little man to David in a voice full of apologies. "I'm the Wizard of Washington Square."

David meant to say "how do you do" back, but he just stood there with his mouth open. Even D. Dog was too surprised to bark.

Don't get left behind!

STARSCAPE

Let the journey begin . . .

THE WIZARD OF
WASHINGTON SQUARE

by JANE YOLEN

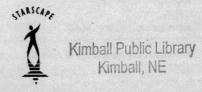

A TOM DOHERTY ASSOCIATES BOOK
NEW YORK

This is a work of fiction. All the characters and events portrayed in this book are either products of the author's imagination or are used fictitiously.

THE WIZARD OF WASHINGTON SQUARE

Cover art by Charles Vess

A Starscape Book
Published by Tom Doherty Associates, LLC
175 Fifth Avenue
New York, NY 10010

www.starscapebooks.com

ISBN 0-765-35016-5
EAN 978-0765-35016-9

First Starscape edition: March 2005

Printed in the United States of America

0 9 8 7 6 5 4 3 2

Magic
and a great deal of Love
For Heidi and Adam

CONTENTS

To Begin Before
the Beginning

Deep in the heart of New York City is a tiny park called Washington Square. It is two blocks long and two blocks wide—which is why it is called a square. On one side, under hovering maple trees, are stone tables inlaid with chess boards. And every nice day in the spring, summer, and fall—and on some bad days as well—the old men of Greenwich Village come out to play.

On the other side of the Square are two tiny playgrounds. And every nice day in the spring, summer, and fall—and on some bad days as well—the children of Greenwich Village come out to play.

Midway between these two sides is a circle. And in the circle is the fountain. Around this circle in the Square, on the fountain's low wall, young men with beards and young women with long hair sit and sun themselves and sing. They do this in all kinds of weather in the spring, summer, and fall. And in the winter, too.

And in the very middle of the fountain, although not very many people know it, lives the Wizard of Washington Square.

It is true, he has often been seen. But because he has a beard and long hair, he is sometimes mistaken for one of the young men and women of the fountain. Or, because his beard and hair are white, it is sometimes thought, by people who do not know better, that he is one of the old men who play chess. And from the back, because he is only three feet high, he is sometimes mistaken for a child.

But he is none of these things. He is a wizard. And he lives in the fountain in the circle in the middle of Washington Square.

DAVID AND LEILAH
AND D. DOG

David walked slowly past the chess players in Washington Square Park. He scuffed his shoes on the pavement and kicked at a fallen leaf. He tried balancing on the low wire fence between the grass and the path, but he kept falling off. Each time he fell off, he looked around, hoping someone would notice him. But the old men kept playing chess and never looked up. Then David tried walking on the grass, right by the KEEP OFF THE GRASS sign. But the policeman on the beat had his back turned.

D. Dog, David's Scottish terrier, raced around him in circles, nipping at his heels.

"D. Dog," thought David unhappily, "is the only one in this whole park—in this whole city—who knows I exist. Who cares." And, feeling very sorry for himself, which was something David could do exceptionally well, he walked slowly toward the fountain in the middle of the square.

As he walked, he pulled a rubber ball out of his back

pocket. It was shiny and unused. "Because," thought David, "I have no one to use it with—except D. Dog." He threw it into the air with ease. His throwing arm had been appreciated in Connecticut, where David had lived until a week ago with his mother and father and three sisters. But it was definitely *not* appreciated in New York—at least, as far as David could prove by the number of friends he had made in a week.

"Not one," David repeated in his thoughts, "not one person cares." And he threw the ball to D. Dog.

D. Dog jumped into the air, snapping at the ball with his teeth, but he missed. The ball hopped, skipped, and bounced over the low retaining wall, rolled past the wading children, and ended up in the center of the fountain. It stopped there, resting against the silver sprayer.

Now D. Dog, as David knew, was a brave dog under almost any circumstance. But water was definitely one of the almosts. As might be guessed from his matted coat, D. Dog was a coward when it came to water. He just stood at the edge of the fountain and barked.

"Well, now you've done it," said David angrily to D. Dog. "How can I get it out unless they turn off the fountain?" By *they*, David meant all the mysterious people who run the parks and clean the playgrounds and turn on the street lamps at dusk.

D. Dog barked again.

David ignored the question in that bark, which meant, "Why don't you fish out the silly ball yourself?" David felt exactly as D. Dog did on a number of subjects—water and dog biscuits, for example. They both hated the first and loved the second. Besides, David was fully dressed.

"Maybe one of the kids will bring it back," David thought. He thought that anyone under the age of ten was a kid. David was eleven, himself.

"I'll get it for you," came a voice from behind them.

David turned around. A girl just about his age was standing there in a bathing suit, carrying a large bath towel. Her black braids were caught up on top of her head, making her look old and wise. A girl, thought David. It would be! He had no use for silly gigglers. Always talking about adventures and never wanting them once they came.

"I'm Leilah and I'm going into the fountain anyway," the girl said. "I'm going to talk to the Wizard."

"Wizard?" David asked, puzzled. Wasn't that just like a girl to think of a story like that. "Wizards only happen in fairy tales. And only *girls* read fairy tales."

"A wizard," said Leilah calmly, "is just exactly who you believe he is."

"Well, who in the world told you that!" asked David.

"The Wizard," said Leilah.

"Of course," said David. "And I suppose this wizard lives in the fountain."

"Where else?" Leilah stepped over the low wall. She dropped her towel in a dry place. Then, avoiding the babies who played in the puddles, stepping over three pails and two shovels, Leilah walked into the middle of the fountain. She knocked three times on the silver sprayer and said something directly into the gurgling water. Or so it seemed to David.

Then Leilah picked up the ball and came out. She deposited it in David's hand.

Shrugging his shoulders in thanks, David looked around to see if anyone was watching them. But no one seemed to care. David wiped the ball on his blue jeans and gave it to D. Dog to carry.

"I certainly didn't see any old wizard," said David. "In fact," he added, "I don't believe there is a wizard at all."

"That's what the Wizard said," Leilah put in. "He said you would never believe in him at all. But I convinced him that seeing is believing. So he promised to meet us by the west side of the Arch." She grinned. "I've never seen him myself," she added.

"Okay," said David nonchalantly. "I wasn't really doing much of anything else." He tried to act reluctant, but actually he was more curious than he would admit. Especially to a girl. Besides, this might be an interesting adventure. Without the girl, of course. She'd never go on with it. It wouldn't be a wizard. Not a real one. David knew they didn't exist. But it might be some interesting nutty old man. And with those thoughts turning over in his head, David joined Leilah in the short walk from the fountain to Washington Square Arch.

It took exactly sixty steps. David counted them out loud as they walked. That included a detour around a hopscotch game and a quick sidestep to avoid a bicycler. David counted out loud to impress Leilah with just how unimpressed he was with meeting her wizard.

When they reached the west side of the Arch, David looked straight up to the top. The Arch rose above them, some five stories high.

"My name is David," said David, squinting into the sun. He didn't want just to stand there saying nothing and it was the first thing that came into his mouth. David often talked that way, bypassing his mind and letting the thoughts just start at his lips. Also, he hated to look at people when he talked to them, which is why he was squinting at the sun. It wasn't very polite but David wasn't very polite either. His father said it came from being an only child. He wasn't, really. He had three older sisters. But since they were five, six, and seven years older, he had always been somewhat spoiled.

"My name is David," David repeated.

"I guessed," said Leilah.

"How did you guess?" David asked the question loudly enough for Leilah to hear, too softly for anyone else to overhear.

Leilah smiled. It was a great open grin. "You *look* like a David!"

David thought that was a pretty stupid thing to say, so he ignored it. "My dog is named D. Dog."

"Why?" asked Leilah.

David shrugged. "Because that's his name."

"Oh."

"I mean, why are you named Leilah or why am I named David? It's just our names."

"I'm named Leilah because it means 'dark as night,'" explained Leilah. She put her arm next to David's. "See, dark as night."

David was beginning to feel silly and started shifting from one leg to the other. "How do you happen to know this wizard?" asked David. "Is he a relative? I've got a lot of crazy relatives too. I have one uncle who thinks he's a telephone pole. He's always having trouble with swallows sitting on his wires."

"Don't be silly," answered Leilah. "The Wizard isn't anybody's relative. He's a wizard. And I am the only *older* person who believes in him. Except you, of course."

"I don't believe in him," David protested hotly.

Leilah just grinned.

"You're crazy!" said David.

Just as he said that, four boys almost his age ran past, shouting. At first David thought they were calling Leilah to play with them. But then he realized they were shouting, "Crazy Leilah, Crazy Leilah," as they passed by. It made David feel both angry and sad. Angry that he boys would gang up on a silly girl—even if she *was* crazy. And sad because he was the one stuck with her.

"Don't pay any attention to them," said Leilah softly. "Two of them are my brothers. And they always call me Crazy Leilah. I made the mistake, you see, of trying to convince *them* about the Wizard. So they don't talk to me any more. But that's okay, because I don't talk to them either."

David didn't say anything.

"It's the babies who know about the Wizard," Leilah continued. "Only because they are real little, and don't talk very well, no one pays any attention to them. That's where most people make a mistake. Children know a lot, only they forget most of it when they grow older. My brothers are only nine and ten, but they've forgotten already. I just have an awful good memory and what my granny calls twenty-twenty ear-hear. You have probably just forgotten about wizards."

David didn't answer, but he doubted that very much. He never forgot anything, that he could remember. Then he said, "I've just moved to New York. That's why I haven't heard of your wizard."

Leilah thought about that for a moment. "Probably," she admitted. After a while she continued. "I listened very carefully to all the baby talk about the Wizard. And then I thought about it," she said. "If all the little ones really believed there was a wizard, well, they couldn't *all* be wrong. So I started to wade. No one over six wades in the fountain. They think they're too old. And no one over twelve does, either. That's the law. But I did. I waded and waded and waded half the summer. Until yesterday he gave himself away."

"How did he do that?" asked David. Even though he didn't believe in the Wizard, he had to admire a girl who had so much patience.

"He uses the silver sprayer like a submarine thing—oh, what do you call it?"

"A periscope," said David, scratching a scab on his arm and trying to pretend he was only half interested.

"A periscope," said Leilah.

"And?" David said, not wanting her to slow down the story.

"And then, yesterday, it moved about."

David looked puzzled. "What moved about?"

"The periscope," said Leilah. "And I said, 'I caught you!' And out of the periscope came a sad voice that said, 'So you have.'"

David scratched D. Dog's head. "If that's all true," David said at last, "where is the Wizard now? And what does he look like?"

"He's . . ." Leilah began, when the small black door in the side of the Arch began to open slowly. David stared as it moved inward and a cave darker than midnight appeared.

From behind the door, into the sunlight, stepped the weirdest little man David had ever seen. He had a long, silky white beard that was parted slightly off center and flowed down to his waist. He was no taller than a four-year-old. He wore a robe of inky blue and a pointed hat that sparkled with stars. The stars weren't just painted on and they weren't rhinestones, either. David could see that they moved, floated in the blue-black space of the hat as though it were a window opening on a night sky.

"How do you do," said the little man to David in a voice full of apologies. "I'm the Wizard of Washington Square."

David meant to say "How do you do" back, but he just stood there with his mouth open. Even D. Dog was too surprised to bark.

The Tunnel
Under the Park

"How do you do. How *do* you do," said the Wizard.

David thought he was terribly polite. Perhaps too polite. And David, not being very polite himself, didn't trust that. But the Wizard was so sincerely sad-looking, David forgot his distrust and put out his hand.

"I'm sorry, my boy, but I can't shake your hand. If I take your hand, we might both be whisked to goodness-knows-where. That's the trouble with magic, you know. There's no containing it. It does what it wants."

"But I thought," said David, "that magicians were the masters of magic."

"Oh, no. You've heard wrong," said the Wizard. "Magic is supreme. It belongs to itself and no other. Only He is Master of Magic."

"He?" said David and Leilah together.

"The Master Mage. The Wonderful Wizard. The Nameless One."

"Does he really not have a name?" asked Leilah.

"Of course he has a name," said the Wizard. "But if we spoke it now, it would call Him to us. And if we called Him for no reason, we'd be vanished! Or even worse."

"What could be worse?" said Leilah.

"Many things," said the Wizard mysteriously.

"Well, what is his name?" asked David, who sometimes got stuck on one track.

"It's—oh, but if I told you, that would be the same as speaking it, wouldn't it?" said the Wizard. "Or would it? I can never remember. I never remember *anything*. That's why I'm here, you know." He gestured to the park.

"You mean here in Washington Square?" asked Leilah.

"No, I mean here in America. They don't believe in magic in America," said the Wizard. "So only second-class magicians are sent here. And oh, I am so very second-class, I'm afraid."

"That's pretty silly," said David. "If no one in America believes in magic, then to convince them, you should send first-class wizards."

"The *very* point I made. The very point!" said the Wizard excitedly. He began to jump up and down. Then he suddenly stopped, shook his head sadly, and said, "But I was voted down. They said it would be a shame to waste good wizards. They said that only the American *children* believe in magic, and only a few at that. The rest see too much television. Ruins their imagination."

"We don't have a television set," said Leilah proudly. "My father would rather have us read books."

"Oh, capital. Capital," said the Wizard. "And do you read?"

"Well," admitted Leilah, "we spend a lot of time at the neighbors'."

"Borrowing books," said the Wizard eagerly.

"Watching television," said Leilah.

David stifled a giggle.

"Oh dear, oh dear," said the Wizard. He looked as though he were going to cry.

David couldn't stand to see anyone cry. Especially a wizard. So, for once in his life, he was tactful and polite. "Tell me all about wizards," he said. "I *really* want to be convinced." He wasn't sure why he said that. After all, he had been the only person in the matinee performance of *Peter Pan* on Wednesday who hadn't clapped for Tinker Bell (including his older sisters, who were usually above such things).

The Wizard's face lighted up. "Of course," he said. "Of course I'll tell you all about—" He looked around suddenly as a rubber ball splatted onto the Arch above his head. "But we can't talk here of important things. It isn't private enough. I know—why don't you come inside with me?" And, with a wide sweep of his hand, he gestured them into the blackness of Washington Square Arch.

David went in after the Wizard. Leilah followed right behind, holding tightly to David's shirttail. D. Dog shivered at their heels. He didn't seem too happy about the whole visit, but he certainly wasn't going to be left behind.

As the four of them cleared the doorway, the door shut behind them with a *clang*.

It took a few minutes for David's eyes to become accustomed to the darkness. It wasn't completely black, because Japanese lanterns were hung at odd intervals along the stone hallway.

"In the Old Country, we use wooden torches," explained the Wizard. "But there is such a shortage of trees in New York City, I have to make do."

"It's very pretty," said Leilah hesitantly.

"It's very dark," muttered David, who was already beginning to regret his politeness and his desire for adventure.

After a few steps, the hallway curved to the left and began to spiral gently downward. There were no stairs, but the stone walk sloped at a slight angle and kept turning and turning left. At each turning was a lantern. As David and Leilah passed, the movement of their bodies caused the lanterns to sway, making colorful, eerie shadows dip and dive along the wall.

David put his hand out along the wall to guide himself. The peculiar angle and turning left all the time were making him slightly dizzy. He was right-handed and so he was feeling very off-balance. The wall was cold and slightly damp. It was covered with patches of something crinkly and velvet to the touch.

"Moss?" thought David, and at that moment Leilah leaned forward, tugged at his shirttail, and hissed to him. David turned his head slightly, trying to keep the Wizard's swiftly moving figure in sight.

"How can there be moss inside Washington Square Arch?" she whispered.

David realized that Leilah had been leaning against the wall too. It made him feel better. So he answered in a voice that sounded braver than he actually felt. "I think," he said, "that we are no longer under the Arch. Did you notice, we've stopped going down. It's mostly flat now."

"No," Leilah admitted. "I guess it happened too slowly."

"Well, it *is* flat now," said David. "I think we're under the fountain. 'Way under. And that might account for the dampness and the moss."

He had no sooner said that when they came around a final turn. The Wizard was nowhere in sight. The tunnel suddenly widened out and where it widened there were three different roads, each marked with a lantern. There was a sign on each of the branches. On the right the sign said TO THE DRAGONRY. On the left was TO THE IRT. And in the middle was a sign that said TO THE WARREN. There was also a sign pointing back the way they had come that read simply WORLD.

"I'd rather not go to the dragonry," said Leilah. "We might be eaten."

"Well, the warren sounds like a place to get lost in," said David. "Guess we'll have to go to the irt, though it does sound ferocious."

"Silly!" said Leilah with a giggle. "That's a subway. The I-R-T." She pronounced each letter separately. "It stands for Interboro Rapid Transit."

"Well, how was I to know?" said David. "I've only lived here a week. To the warren, then," he said. "I'd rather get lost than eaten."

THE WIZARD'S WARREN

D. Dog gave three short staccato barks and ran through David's legs. He raced down the middle tunnel, the one marked TO THE WARREN. Just as he reached what must have been the end, a door opened and David and Leilah saw light. Bright yellow light.

They ran quickly after D. Dog and reached the open door together. They peered in.

"Well, and what took you so long?" the Wizard asked.

David and Leilah stood at the entrance with their mouths wide open. Inside the doorway was another world.

The Wizard sat in a large velvet-cushioned oak chair in front of a tremendous table. The table was as long as a large door and had nine sturdy legs, each ending in a claw. One claw clutched a wooden ball and, at odd moments, it would suddenly roll the ball to another leg. Then that claw would snatch the ball and stand very proudly on it. In this way, every few minutes, the table would take on a slightly different tilt. Each time the game began again, all the beakers and bowls and pitchers and jars on top of the table—for the table was littered with glassware and crockery—would jangle and clank. But, surprisingly, nothing was ever broken.

The Wizard seemed unaware of the moving table and sat, with his legs crossed, on the velvet-cushioned chair.

On the wall behind the Wizard was a large tapestry. It seemed to be woven of glistening thread. Yet it was like no painting or tapestry David had ever seen. Though he could never quite catch them moving, the figures of the tapestry were in new and different positions every time David looked. When he stared directly at the tapestry, there was absolutely no movement at all. But the minute he looked away, from the corner of his eye he seemed to see a blurred, frantic scurrying.

"You'll never catch them," said the Wizard to David. "And it's best not to try."

But whether the Wizard meant the table legs or the tapestry figures, David didn't know. So he started to walk over to look at the tapestry more closely, and nearly bumped his head on a large object that jutted down from the ceiling. It had two handles and an eyepiece.

Leilah, who hadn't left his side, whispered, "That must be the periscope."

"Then I was right," David whispered back. "We *are* under the fountain!"

The Wizard shook his head. "Not fair," he said. "Not fair at all. Most impolite. First you stand and stare as though you had never seen a wizard's warren before, and then you whisper in company."

"But we never *have* seen a wizard's warren before," began Leilah apologetically.

"Oh, yes. I forgot," said the Wizard, a little sadly. "I'm always forgetting. I'm always forgetting, especially, that I'm in America."

"Maybe you're wishing that you weren't in America," said Leilah. "That could account for the forgetting."

"I doubt it," said the Wizard. "I doubt it very much. I even forget things I want to remember—like spells and incantations. And when I remember how to start them, I forget how to make them stop."

"How very sad for you," said Leilah.

"Maybe you could take a correspondence course to improve your memory," said David. "I've seen some advertised in magazines."

"I once tried," said the Wizard, "but the postman never knew where to deliver my mail. So he dropped it in the wastebasket near the Arch. I didn't beat the garbage truck to it in the morning. Somewhere in New York City there is a garbageman with an excellent memory. But not me. Not the Wizard of Washington Square." And he began to cry, with his head on his arms on the tilting oak table.

David and Leilah looked at each other uneasily.

"Well, we'll just have to help you, that's all," said Leilah. "Won't we, David?"

David shrugged his shoulders. He had no idea how to help a second-class wizard. He didn't even know how to help a first-class wizard, though he doubted that a first-class wizard would need any help at all. Instead, David bent down and held on to D. Dog's collar, for the terrier was trying to grab the wooden ball from one of the table's claws.

The Wizard looked up, took a handkerchief from the air, and wiped his eyes with it. Then he snapped his fingers, and the handkerchief disappeared.

David wondered how a second-class wizard could do such a thing.

As though he had read David's mind, the Wizard answered. "I can do simple things, like prestidigitation, but—"

"Presti—what?" asked David.

"Prestidigitation. Sleight-of-hand tricks," said the Wizard. "It comes from *presto* meaning nimble and *digit* meaning finger."

"Oh," said David, "I see." But he didn't.

"Magicians are presti-whatchmacallits," explained Leilah.

David's eyes lighted up. "Oh, magicians," he said.

"Magicians! Bah!" said the Wizard.

"Why *bah?*" asked Leilah.

"Magicians are imitators, not creators. They are fakers. They make tricks to fool your eye. But that is all it is, trickery. What I do—when I can remember how to do it—is real."

"You mean you really made that handkerchief disappear?" asked Leilah.

"Certainly," replied the Wizard. "But a magician would make it disappear *up his sleeve.*"

"Well," said David, "if you can't make it as a wizard, you could always be a first-class magician. No one would ever figure out your tricks."

"I would rather be a *third*-class wizard than the best magician in the world," said the Wizard. His eyes were fierce. David was sorry he had ever spoken.

"Is there such a thing as a third-class wizard?" asked Leilah quickly.

"No, I'm the lowest there is. So low, in fact, that I have to live in a warren."

"That's pretty low down," agreed David.

"It is. It is," said the Wizard. "Wizards prefer high towers with vast views. Now, my tutor, the great Greywether, had an imposing tower on the Welsh Pembroke coast. His weather spells were world-famous. But wizardry fell on bad times for a while in the British Isles. He was forced to rent his tower to the Crown for a lighthouse. Since the war, though, he's made a comeback. He even has the support of a local coven."

"Coven?" the children asked together.

"Witches."

"Oh," said David, nudging Leilah. But Leilah seemed to believe it all. And it did seem a bit odd, the table and tapestry and all. Perhaps, David thought, it would be a good idea to find out more about this wizardry business before dismissing it. Just in case.

"What do wizards do?" asked David. "I mean, besides taking handkerchiefs out of the air?"

"I'm supposed to help people with their problems. You know—find lost sheep, make love potions, break spells. That sort of thing. But in America, no one wants to consult a wizard. They write to the papers instead. I was put in the small towns first but people just thought I was a beatnik. Then I tried San Francisco. Chicago. Detroit. I was put in jail while passing through Georgia. Now I'm in New York, the biggest, most crowded city in America. And it's my last chance. If I can't help someone soon and prove my worth as a wizard, I'm liable to be demoted to an elf. Or a troll. Or simply dematerialized." He put his head on the table and started crying again. The two ends of his beard were soon dripping tears onto the floor.

Leilah turned to David urgently. "We can't let him go on like this," she said. "What can we do?"

"I'm not a wizard. How should I know?" said David. But Leilah looked at him so sharply that he added, "Help him help someone."

"You're right," said Leilah. "Isn't he?" she asked the Wizard.

"Yes," the Wizard answered in a voice that was more of a sigh than anything else. Then he snuffled and wiped his eyes with his long white beard. The beard sparkled with stars for an instant and then was dry.

"You should use your handkerchief," scolded Leilah.

"I don't have one," complained the Wizard.

"You took one from the air last time," David said.

"So I did," said the Wizard. "So I did. I forgot."

"Then the problem is," said Leilah, "to help him to help someone so that he can be sent back to the Old Country."

"Or fix his memory," added David.

"Or both," said the Wizard quietly.

"Whichever is easier," said Leilah.

"I would imagine," David said, "since his memory seems

to be full of more holes than a butterfly net, and since I can't think of anyone who needs help, that we should just concentrate on getting him back to the Old Country. Buy him a ticket, I suppose."

"No money," said Leilah.

"If he were a good wizard, he could make his own money," said David. "And then give it to the poor. That way he'd be helping people and also financing his trip home."

The Wizard looked up from the table. He shook his head and the last of the tears twinkled off his beard. "I can't just *go* back to the Old Country. I have to be recalled. For helping someone. And that someone has to need me. I can't just give away my magic, or money made by magic. It's part of being a wizard. It's called the Rule of Need. And as for my memory, it's no use. I've forgotten so much, I forget how much I've forgotten."

"Well, since you're here in America, they can't object to things being done the American way, can they?" asked Leilah.

"What do you mean?" asked the Wizard.

"Well, it's a kind of custom, at least in the Village, when there is a need, to have people sign a petition. So, we could get up a petition saying we *need* the Wizard to go home."

"A petition?" said David. "You mean with names?"

"I've never heard of one *without* names," Leilah said.

"But who on earth would sign such a thing?" asked the Wizard. "Presuming, of course, you mean on earth. One never knows with magic."

Leilah grinned. "Everyone in the Village is always signing

petitions. For stopping bombs and starting committees. For closing streets and opening clubs. I know how it's done. My Mom and Dad do it all the time. All you do is set up a table with pencils and a piece of paper with large words on the top. And then plenty of space to sign below. Then we'd be *asking* that you be sent home."

The Wizard smiled.

"But no one will sign," said David. "I mean, when they read what it's about, they'll think we're crazy."

"Nobody ever *reads* what a petition is about," replied Leilah. "They just sign."

David shook his head. "If you did that in Connecticut, you'd be arrested."

The Wizard groaned. He remembered the jail in Georgia.

"If the police come to stop us," said Leilah, "we'll get twice as many signatures, and people will help us out. I mean, that's the way it's done in Greenwich Village."

The Wizard smiled again and stood up.

David shrugged. "You ought to know," he said. "You've lived here long enough. But where will we set it up?"

"By the outdoor art show, of course," said Leilah. "Tomorrow morning. Sunday. Early. That's where everyone will be."

The Wizard laughed out loud. "It might work," he said. He clicked his heels together and a table leg rolled the ball under him. When he came down, he slipped on the ball and fell. He picked up the ball and got heavily to his feet. Then he put the ball on top of the table in a glass jar.

"Nasty thing," he said, kicking at the table leg and missing. "You'll just have to do without for a while." Then he smiled at the children, and at D. Dog too. "But it must be late, so perhaps you'd better go home for supper."

"What time is it?" asked David and Leilah together.

The Wizard went over to the periscope and looked through the eyepiece. "According to the Judson Church clock, it's nearly six o'clock."

"Oh, oh," said David. "I'm late."

"Me too," said Leilah. All at once she narrowed her eyes. "But there *isn't* any clock on Judson Church."

"Of course not," said the Wizard.

"But *you* said . . ." said David. "I mean, you looked through the periscope and said . . ."

"Exactly," said the Wizard. "This is a *were*-scope."

"Is that like a werewolf?" asked David.

"No," said the Wizard. "But this scope shows things as you wish they *were*, not as they actually *are*. And since it can't see as far as the Jefferson Market Courthouse Clock, I just wish the clock to Judson Church and the scope shows it there."

"Wow!" said David.

Leilah smiled her slow smile. But then the worry lines on her forehead showed. "But is it correct? The time, I mean?"

"Oh yes," said the Wizard. "At least it is if the real clock is."

"Then I really am late," said Leilah.

"Me too," said David.

They both said good-by and ran out the door with D. Dog at their heels. As they started up the tunnel, the Wizard called after them, "Don't forget the petition. I'll be waiting here. Just knock on the sprayer and then on the door."

"We won't forget," called out David. "But don't you."

"I never forget things," said the Wizard, "if I try not to remember them."

At least, that was what it sounded like to David. But the door slammed shut and cut off the rest of the Wizard's words. And soon they were out in the Square again, blinking in the fading sunlight.

A PERFECT DAY FOR SIGNING

The next day, Sunday, was a glorious day. The sun was high overhead but a gentle, cooling breeze blew east from the Hudson River.

In Washington Square Park, the young men with beards and the young women with long hair were sitting or standing or sprawling around the fountain in small clumps. They were playing guitars and banjos and singing.

David circled slowly around the fountain. As he walked, he marveled how the song from one group would slowly fade as he passed, gradually blending with a new song from the group he was approaching. It was like switching stations on a giant radio, David thought.

Little children were screaming in the playgrounds, happy Sunday screams. And families on their way to or from church strolled by to watch the artists set up exhibits on the walls and gates of brownstone houses near the Square. And if the strollers stared more at the artists than at their art, it was to be expected.

All in all, it was a perfect day for signing petitions. At least that was what Leilah said when she met David. They knocked on the sprayer in the fountain and then walked to the Arch and knocked at the door. Leilah was carrying the pencils and papers they needed. The Wizard was going to supply the table.

"I hope," said David, "that he doesn't supply that walking table of his. Or else we are liable to lose the petition and pencils as well as our case."

"Our case?" asked Leilah.

"The one in court when the police arrest us," said David. He knelt down to scratch D. Dog's ears. He didn't want Leilah to notice that his knees were shaking a bit. In fact, he hadn't been feeling well all morning. He had tried to convince his mother that he was sick and should stay in bed. But his sisters were all at camp and his mother had a meeting to go to, so she merely thrust a dollar in his pocket and advised him to eat lightly. What fun was it to stay in bed if you had to get up to get your own juice? So David had come out to the park hoping that Leilah might have forgotten the whole idea of petitions. After all, it was one thing to visit a wizard in his warren. It was another to bring the wizard into your world.

David looked up. "Do you think he'll wear normal clothes?" he asked.

"What do you mean by normal?"

"You can't call the clothes he was wearing yesterday normal," said David.

"They were perfectly normal," said Leilah, "for a wizard."

"That's what I mean," said David.

"What's wrong with you?" asked Leilah. "Scared?"

"Of course not!" David said hotly. "It's just—it's just that I've never done anything like this before."

"Well, neither have I," said Leilah. "But in the Village, a lot of things happen that never happened before and no one who lives here pays any attention. It's just *tourists* who get all shook." The way she said *tourists* made David promise himself that he would never be one, much less act like one.

"Like what happens?" asked David, standing up.

"Like—like happenings," said Leilah.

"Oh fine, that says a lot. Happenings that never happened before happen to happen here."

Leilah shook her head. "No, really. Happenings are things that people plan. Nutty things. Wild things. Like people dressing up as babies and drinking bottles of *milk*. Or dancing with camels. Or shoving whipped-cream pies in someone's face and then licking it off. And people pay admission to see them. It's like a show, only you never know ahead of time what is going to happen. So, it's called a *happening*."

"Sounds stupid," said David.

"It is, a bit," Leilah admitted.

"Say, maybe somebody will think that we're a happening," said David. He began to laugh.

"Maybe," said Leilah.

Just then the door in the archway opened inward. The

cave, dark as doom, appeared. And from far away, stars began to appear, flickering on and off like erratic fireflies. As the stars got closer, David realized they were on the Wizard's hat. They kept appearing and disappearing as the Wizard turned his head.

"Now why is he looking backward all the time?" thought David. And then he understood. The Wizard was holding the wooden ball and coaxing the table. Reluctantly it trotted behind him, like a stubborn donkey led by a carrot.

David ran to the Arch and blocked the doorway. D. Dog growled at his heels. "Oh, please," he said, "you can't bring that out. If someone saw, we might be arrested. . . ."

"My dear boy," said the Wizard, "I've never been arrested here before. And I always take the table out for its Sunday constitutional. We usually do it at midnight, when there aren't many children about. It will go after any bouncing ball it sees."

"Its constitutional?" exclaimed David.

"Why, this table needs exercise as much as any dog. After all, it has more legs, hasn't it?" said the Wizard.

And that was that.

With some misgivings David and D. Dog followed Leilah behind the Wizard as he paraded the table around the park. Just as Leilah had predicted, none of the old men or the children or the young men with beards or the young women with long hair noticed. And the policemen were too busy buying ice-cream cones from the vendor at the corner of the Square. One fat lady fainted when she saw them, but then it was her first time in New York. And since she fainted in front of four native New Yorkers who were arguing about city politics, no one noticed her or bothered to pick her up. Finally she found some smelling salts in her pocketbook, dusted herself off, and went home to Iowa where she told everyone about the sights of New York and no one believed her.

Eventually the table must have had enough exercise, because the Wizard led them out of the park, through the Arch, and onto a block where the art show was in progress.

"This is fine," said Leilah approvingly. "We ought to get a lot of signatures here."

The Wizard signaled the table and it settled on the corner of the block. Then Leilah spread the papers on the table, putting pencils within easy reach of any interested signers.

"If we're lucky," Leilah said, "someone who is running for office will be down shaking hands. We can get them to sign, too. It's always best to have some of them—stop it!"

Leilah ended in a shriek as the table stepped on her foot.

The Wizard smiled apologetically and kicked at the table leg. He missed, but the table settled down. "Sometimes it gets in its own way," he said. "Too many legs, you know. Thank you," he added, as two bearded young men with guitars stopped to sign the petition before they entered the park.

"See?" said Leilah smugly.

David shrugged.

A half-dozen well-dressed people passed the table without signing. They stared at the Wizard's clothes and one lady giggled.

"See?" said David smugly.

"Tourists," said Leilah. "They don't know any better."

A skinny man with eyeglasses that pinched his nose and a long, well-waxed moustache bent over the table. He looked at its legs. He knocked on its top. He examined its underside. This so irritated the table that it kicked the man in the shins. "Ow!" screamed the man and hopped up and down on one foot for a while, which made his glasses pop off his nose and his Adam's apple wobble about. Then he bent down to see who had kicked him. There was nothing within reach but two table legs, so he stood up and looked around. Then he turned to the Wizard.

"You," he thundered.

"Me?" squeaked the Wizard, who was not used to being thundered at.

"You," said the skinny man, putting his glasses back on his nose. "You must sell me this table. It's a rare piece. Name your price."

"Oh, I can't. It's been in my family for generations. Ever since the Good Old Days," said the Wizard.

"What is your price?" shouted the man. "I know you Villagers. You'll do anything for a price. So name your price."

"I'm not selling," said the Wizard.

"We'll see," said the skinny man. "Here's my card. Call me when you are ready to sell." He laid his card on the table and started to walk off. As he did, the table leg on the corner reached out and tripped him.

The man turned around and his glasses popped off again. But the only one close to him was D. Dog. Furiously the man poked D. Dog with his umbrella, which made the terrier scream and run under the table.

"Hey, you can't do that to my dog!" shouted David, but the man walked off without a word.

David started to run after him, but Leilah caught his arm. "We always know where to find him if we want him," Leilah said, and held up the man's card. It said *Joseph Pickwell, Decorator. VIP Interiors, 190 East 58th Street.* "The petition is more important."

The Wizard nodded.

David settled back. He looked at the papers spread out on the table. "And he didn't even sign," David said in disgust.

SWINGING STATUES

"Fifty-seven," said Leilah, after a slow hour had gone by. She counted the names on the petition again. "Fifty-seven signatures. That's including you and me and D. Dog's paw-print."

"Is that good or bad?" asked David.

"Good, I think," said Leilah.

"Then let's stop for a while and get an ice cream or something," suggested David.

They packed up the pencils and petition and the Wizard put them under his pointed hat. Then they sent the table back to the warren. "It doesn't care for ice cream," the Wizard explained. "So we certainly won't hurt its feelings."

"How can you hurt a table's feelings?" asked David.

"It's easy. I do it all the time. They're extremely sensitive," said the Wizard. And though David wanted to pursue the matter, the Wizard would say no more.

After they got their ice cream, with the Wizard treating,

the three walked over to the maples and sat down. The Wizard leaned his back against the KEEP OFF THE GRASS sign.

David had barely gotten to his third lick of cherry vanilla when a very large policeman started yelling at them from the sidewalk. "Hey, can't you kids read?"

"Read what?" asked the Wizard, turning around.

"The sign, wise guy," said the policeman, who was tired of being in the hot sun. Besides, he didn't like being stationed in Washington Square where, as he had told his wife that morning at breakfast, "It's not only hard to tell the girls from the boys, it's hard to tell the people from the animals."

"This sign?" asked the Wizard, pointing to the one he was leaning against.

"That sign!" said the policeman, wiping his forehead. His normally rosy cheeks were even pinker in the heat.

"Oh, yes," said the Wizard, squinting at the sign and taking a pair of wire-rimmed glasses from an enormous pocket in his robe. "It says 'Enjoy the grass, that's what it's here for.'"

"Okay, wise guy," shouted the policeman. Shouting was his normal tone of voice. It was loud enough to have interested three bearded young men, a teen-aged girl with long beads and dark glasses, and an old man who carried his possessions everywhere in a paper bag. They all came over to see what was happening. "Okay, wise guy," shouted the policeman again, "I'm going to—" He stopped and stared. The Wizard had moved away from the sign. And it was true. The sign, somehow, did say ENJOY THE GRASS, THAT'S WHAT IT'S HERE FOR.

"Wow, dig!" said the three boys, and they threw themselves on the grass and rolled in it, kicking up their heels. The girl pushed up her dark glasses onto her head and smiled a very slow smile. The old man bent down and plucked a few blades of grass and put them in his paper bag. And the policeman wandered off mumbling to himself, "I know that sign did say 'Keep off the grass.'"

"How did you do that?" asked David.

"Do what?" asked the Wizard, who was puzzled by all the fuss.

"Change the sign," David said. "It *did* say 'Keep off the grass' when we sat down."

"I don't know," said the Wizard.

"If you could only figure out how you do things like that—and the handkerchief—you could be a first-class wizard," said Leilah.

The Wizard looked thoughtful. "I suppose so," he said. "But the more I think about the magic, the less able I am to do it."

"Then it's easy!" said David. "Just don't think about it at all."

"I'm afraid that's impossible," said the Wizard. "It's just like the story old Greywether used to tell his apprentices. For years, he said, the alchemists had been pestering him to tell them the secret of turning lead into gold. Finally he was so annoyed with them, he jokingly told them that all they had to do was to put the lead into a huge vat over a roaring fire and stir it, all the while not thinking of a pink hippocampus. Well, of course, from that moment on, not a single alchemist could stir a lead-filled cauldron without thinking of a pink hippocampus, so none of them ever were able to turn lead into gold."

"What's a hippocampus?" David whispered to Leilah.

"You've missed the whole point of the story," said Leilah, who didn't want to admit she didn't know what a hippocampus was.

"So," continued the Wizard, "I'm afraid that not thinking of magic is as impossible for me as remembering correctly. I guess I was just born to be a second-class wizard." He sighed. "Never to make magic properly. Never to have fun. . . ."

"Oh well, you needn't count on magic for having fun," said Leilah brightly. "All you have to do is play games."

"But I don't know how," said the Wizard.

David said helpfully, "But it wouldn't be hard to remember how to play the games you played when you were little—er, littler."

"I never did," said the Wizard. "Play games, that is. Wizards don't. Too busy learning magic."

"Well, from the amount of magic you learned," said David, "you might just as well have been playing games and having fun."

"David, what a mean thing to say," Leilah whispered.

"He's right, I'm afraid," said the Wizard. "And I guess it's too late to learn now."

"Nonsense," said Leilah. "It's never too late to learn how to play." And she reached out to take the Wizard by the hand. "Let's go."

"Oh, don't touch, don't touch, child," said the Wizard. "The magic. Remember the magic."

"Oh pooh on the magic. If you can't remember it, why should we?" said David, and he and Leilah grabbed the Wizard and hauled him quickly to his feet.

They dragged him, his beard wagging from side to side, to the sidewalk near the Arch. There Leilah drew a hopscotch pattern on the pavement with yellow chalk. And after one time through for practice and one time through for real, the Wizard was beating them both by four squares.

"I'm not so sure that teaching him to play was such a good idea after all," said David, who was sometimes a sore loser. "Let's play something else."

"All right," said Leilah, who was a bit put out herself. "Let's play swinging statues."

"How does that go?" asked the Wizard. His face was flushed with pleasure and the heat. He liked winning at hopscotch and hated to stop.

"You take turns being It," David began.

"And," interrupted Leilah, "It swings everyone in the game around and around. When It lets go, you have to fall in a funny position and hold it, still as a statue, while It swings the next person and looks everyone over. Whoever It chooses as being the best, becomes It in turn."

"Does anyone win?" asked the Wizard eagerly.

"No," said David. "It's not like hopscotch."

"I'm not so sure . . ." said the Wizard. But before he could protest further, Leilah announced, "I'll be It first."

She grabbed David's hand and started to swing him,

singing tunelessly, "Swinging here, swinging there, swinging statues everywhere." At the last syllable, she let him go and he spun around and landed on his knees like a giant praying mantis. Next Leilah grabbed D. Dog and swung him, too. The terrier landed on his back and lay there, playing dead. Then she grabbed the Wizard, who started to protest about the magic. But when nothing happened, he closed his eyes, enjoyed the spinning, and wound up with his arms spread wide like airplane wings.

"I think the Wizard is best," said Leilah quickly.

"What's so good about him?" grumbled David.

"Shut up," Leilah hissed at him. "He's never played before. So let him think he's doing a good job."

"He already beat us both at hopscotch," said David grudgingly. "I don't think he deserves any special consideration at all."

"Well, I'm It, and I say the Wizard is best." She called out to the Wizard, who was beginning to twirl his beard like a propeller. "Come on. You're It."

"I was just getting ready for the takeoff," said the Wizard. "Oh well, guess I'll just have to cut the motor." His beard stopped twirling, his arms lowered, and the Wizard stepped over to take his turn at being It.

Tentatively he took David's hand and swung David around. "Swinging here, swinging there, swinging statues everywhere," he chanted. And then he let go.

Next he took D. Dog by the paw. He had abandoned himself to the game and forgotten all about magic. The terrier had been chewing on the grass and a small dandelion was stuck to the corner of his mouth. The Wizard's eyes glowed. The stars on his hat seemed to wink in and out. He closed his eyes and started to sing the tuneless "Swinging here, swinging there, swinging statues every—Oh dear!"

"What is it?" asked David from a crouched position, his head between his knees.

"I knew it would happen. I knew the magic would come when we least expected it." The Wizard's voice cracked in midsentence.

David straightened up. Leilah came over.

There, on the sidewalk before them, was a marble statue of a Scotty.

"Why, what is that?" asked Leilah.

"I'm afraid it's David's dog," said the Wizard. "And he's a real statue now."

WHAT·THE TAPESTRY SAW

I don't understand," said Leilah. "You mean a *real* statue?" She bent over to look at D. Dog more closely. It was true. Each detail of his nose and tail and whiskers and every single hair was visible. Even the dandelion in his mouth. But it was all in polished white marble.

"But how could you?" asked David with a wail. "How could you do such a thing! He's my dog. My only dog."

"I wish I knew how I did it," said the Wizard. "I mean, if I knew, I could undo it easily. But I warned you about touching. Really I did. It's the touching that does it."

"Well, you didn't warn us enough," said David belligerently. "How were we to know just how magic the touching could be? I thought it was just—you know, handkerchiefs in the air and signs. I didn't know you meant to change my dog into . . . into . . ." and embarrassingly enough, David started to cry. Right there in the park in front of a girl.

"I didn't mean to do it," the Wizard said. He started to

pat David comfortingly on the back and caught himself in time. Looking at his own hand, he mumbled, "I must *try* to remember."

So Leilah did the patting instead. But David was not to be comforted. He picked up the marble dog and started slowly out of the park. He trudged past hopscotch games and children playing tag, past an old man with a chess set under his arm and a mother wheeling twins in an oversized carriage.

"Wait," called the Wizard, "maybe I could do something to help. At least I could try."

But David did not even turn back to look.

"Perhaps you've done too much already," said Leilah. She meant it to be consoling, but somehow it came out wrong.

They watched as David came to the street, the statue cradled in his arms. Just as he started to cross, a taxi pulled up beside him and a man leaned out. He grabbed the statue from David's hands and thrust something in its place. Then he closed the door and drove off uptown in the taxi. Stunned, David just stood there. And when he finally started yelling, it was too late. The taxi was lost in the stream of Sunday traffic that was heading up Fifth Avenue.

Leilah and the Wizard raced over.

"Come back, thief! Come back with my dog! Stop! Please. Oh, please," David was shouting.

"It's no use," said Leilah. "He can't possibly hear you. But who was it? And why did he take the statue?"

"I don't know," said David. "He just drove up and said, 'Beautiful. I'll take it.' And handed me this."

David opened his hand. In it was a twenty-dollar bill.

"Didn't you recognize him?" asked the Wizard.

"Recognize him? Why should I recognize him?" asked David.

"That was our old friend of the table," said the Wizard.

David's face brightened a bit. "You're right!"

"See, you *do* remember things," said Leilah.

"Why, so I do—sometimes," said the Wizard, quite pleased with himself. "And it wasn't difficult either."

"But what am I to do now?" asked David. "Before, I at least had a statue of D. Dog. Now I have nothing. Nothing at all."

"What makes it worse," the Wizard added, "is that with the statue I might have been able to do something." He sighed and rubbed his left hand slowly with his right. "But without it, I'm afraid there is nothing I can do at all. It's the touching, you know."

"We could buy back the statue if we only knew where to find the man," said Leilah. "But we don't."

"Oh yes we do," said David. "He gave us his card, remember? The Wizard put it in his hat."

"I did?" asked the Wizard.

"What a memory!" said David.

"Well, let's look in his hat, then," Leilah said.

The Wizard took off his hat and put his hand inside. He felt around for several moments. Then he pulled out a pickle, two rabbits, a white pigeon, three paper clips, a chewed-on pencil stub, a half-eaten chocolate bar, and five rubber bands.

"That's it, I'm afraid," said the Wizard.

"But where are today's petition and the man's card?" asked Leilah.

"I don't know," said the Wizard.

"Oh, fine," said David.

"However, if we wait a week or two, they may turn up. Sometimes things get a bit lost in the hat. Something about a time differential. Take that pickle. It was from last Wednesday's lunch. And the chocolate bar I put in there sometime in May. And it's not even melted or stale. Imagine that!" the Wizard said as he unwrapped the bar and offered a bit to David and Leilah. When they refused, he took a bite and continued, "I'm sure nothing gets lost in the hat permanently."

"But while we wait, the man might mail the statue to Australia, or drop it and break it, or anything," said David.

"He's right, you know," said Leilah. And then in a scolding voice she added, "Besides, if you knew things get lost for days in your hat, why did you put the card in there?"

"How was I to know we were to need it today? And as for the petition—well, I forgot."

"You sure do forget at the worst possible times," said David.

Suddenly the Wizard looked jubilant. "But we don't need the card as long as we have the tapestry in the warren," he said. "I just remembered. We can watch from there."

"What do you mean?" David and Leilah asked together.

"Never mind. It would take too long to explain. Just follow me." And with that, the Wizard took off toward the Arch at a fast rolling trot.

David and Leilah had no difficulty this time keeping up with the Wizard. Even the twists of the dark tunnel were surprisingly familiar. They giggled as they passed the four signposts, and poked each other with their elbows at each turning. David was immensely pleased, even though he was afraid for D. Dog, for it suddenly occurred to him that this was, indeed, an adventure. Even if he was sharing it with a girl.

In less than three minutes they were at the door, which the Wizard opened by giving a large gold ring a hard tug.

"Name, rank, and serial number," said the ring.

"I got it at army surplus," explained the Wizard.

David ran immediately to the tapestry hanging on the wall but it was empty. Or rather, it had a delicate floral border but the center was just a field of royal blue with nothing on it.

"What happened to the pictures?" he asked. "The ones we saw yesterday?"

"Oh, I finished that story," said the Wizard. "It was very dull, really. The ugly but brilliant prince married a lovely but rather simple princess and they lived affluently ever after. Not like the good old stories. Ah, the Middle Ages, those were the days!"

"What do you mean, 'finished'?" asked Leilah, joining David at the tapestry.

"The tapestry will let you watch anyone you want to."

"I want to see the man who stole my dog."

"Then," said the Wizard, "you have to sit in that chair." He pointed to the oak chair he had been sitting in when the children had first entered the warren on Saturday. This time they noticed that it had a cushion covered in the same royal blue material of the tapestry.

David sat down in the chair. He felt that he was sinking, sinking deep into the chair . . . that the chair would take care of him, love him, and cherish him. He felt that, in turn, he loved and cherished the chair.

"It does that to you the first time," said the Wizard when he noticed the sweet smile on David's face. "It likes to try to overwhelm you."

"You talk about the chair the same way you talk about your walking table," observed Leilah.

"Of course. They're in the same family. First cousins, actually. So they have a lot in common." The Wizard chuckled. "You should have seen their grandsire. A real brute of an oak."

"Hey, what about my statue?" said David in a small, faraway voice. He was still slightly overcome by the chair's maternal authority.

"Just think about the man and about your statue. What they look like. How and where you last saw them," said the Wizard. "But whatever you do, don't look at the tapestry until the signal is given. That particular chair is very bashful about showing half-finished work. If you peek, it might be weeks before it will show anyone anything again."

"But what's the signal?" asked David.

"Oh you'll know it when you hear it," said the Wizard. "It's different for everyone."

So David concentrated on the statue of D. Dog, the polished marble surface of the little terrier, the tiny dandelion sticking out of its mouth. And he thought about the man, too, his skinny face with the monocle and the waxed moustache. He pictured in his mind the taxi driving up Fifth Avenue with the man's skinny head looking straight in front of him, and the tips of his moustache sticking out on either side.

As David sat there thinking about all this, he felt tiny fingers probing at his mind as if tearing off little pieces of memory gently, oh so gently. It was a kind of brain tickle, and he started to giggle.

Suddenly he heard a familiar voice right in his own head— it was his mother's voice. It said, "You may look now, David."

And he looked.

There on the tapestry was the skinny man riding in the taxi. Balanced on his lap was the statue of D. Dog. The man was looking very angry and was shaking his fist at the driver, who had his shoulders hoisted in a shrug. Traffic, it seemed, was very slow. David could just make out a street sign. It said "58th Street."

"Will it show us anything more?" asked David. "I mean, that's not much help really."

"Only if you don't watch it change."

So David and Leilah and the Wizard turned away for a few moments. And when they turned back, the tapestry showed the man getting out of the taxi. Obviously he had given a very small tip. This time the driver was shaking *his* fist.

The three watchers turned away again. When they turned back, quickly this time, they saw the man going into a shop that said *J. Pickwell. VIP Interiors. 190 East 58th Street.* He carried the statue under his arm.

"That's it. I remember now," said Leilah. "Joseph Pickwell."

"He certainly is well named," commented the Wizard.

"Pickleface Pickwell," said David, jumping out of the chair, "here I come. Ready or not. I'm coming to get my dog!"

THE IRT

Wait for me," said Leilah to David. He stopped at the door with his hand almost on the terra-cotta knob. The knob had an eye drawn on it. It blinked as David's hand touched it and two big tears squeezed out.

"I'm afraid you are hurting the knob," said the Wizard.

"Everything around here gets hurt too easily," said David. "Chairs, table, doorknobs. And they get plenty of sympathy. But I'm in real trouble. Or my dog is. That's kind of the same thing. The least you could do is offer to help."

"You mean, you need me?" asked the Wizard in a peculiar voice.

David looked puzzled.

"Of course he does," said Leilah quickly.

"I've done it. I've done it. *I've done it*!" cried the Wizard. "I've found someone who needs me."

"Well, stop shouting and clicking your heels," said David, for the Wizard was doing just that. "And come on along. I suppose I need you. I need *all* the help I can get."

"Oh, but that will be impossible," said the Wizard.

"What do you mean, impossible?" asked David. "A minute ago you were excited about helping. So help."

"I can't go out of my territory. And my territory is the Village. It's very specific. It's in my contract. Once you settle in a territory, you have to stick. I might get in the way of another wizard."

"You mean there are other second-class wizards running around New York City?" asked Leilah.

"No," said the Wizard.

"Then what's stopping you?" asked David.

"It's the rule. Rule number two, that is. Rule number one is the Rule of Need. And rule number two is the Rule of Territory."

"Well, if there are no more wizards in New York, it's a stupid rule," said David impatiently.

"It's a very old rule," said the Wizard. "It was made in the days when there were a great many wizards and the New World had not yet been discovered. Nor a good deal of the Old either, for that matter. And like many rules, it has outlived its usefulness, I'm afraid."

"Then you should change the rule," said David.

"Yes," said Leilah. "Protest. March against it."

The Wizard sighed. "If I were younger, I might. I think I'm too old and too second-class to try."

"So how can you help David?" asked Leilah. "I mean, it's one thing to know he needs you and another—and more important—to help. Rules or no rules."

"I'll watch you on the tapestry and check my books and mix up a good-speed spell. Or is it a God-speed? Perhaps it makes a difference with the kind of gods you believe in. Once there was no problem. We all believed in the same thing. You do believe in something, don't you?"

"I don't believe in you," mumbled David under his breath as he went out the door. He was tired of arguing. Every minute was precious to him.

But Leilah turned and said sweetly, "Of course we do."

"Well, then, you two hurry along. And take the turning to the IRT. It's probably fastest. And don't get lost."

"Don't worry," said Leilah. "I'd hate to end up in the dragonry by mistake."

"Oh—that!" said the Wizard and he started to laugh, his face wrinkling like a white raisin. "There are no dragons here. That's just a sign I brought with me from the Old Country. No, that tunnel leads to the New York City sewer system."

"That's a relief," said Leilah. "I sure wouldn't have wanted to meet up with a dragon," and she ran out after David.

The Wizard closed the door after them, muttering absentmindedly, "No—no dragons at all. Just the great white alligators that live in the sewer."

But David and Leilah were already far down the tunnel and didn't hear what he said.

When Leilah caught up with David, she explained, "We'll

take the turning to the IRT and go by subway. It's the fastest way there."

"Are you sure?" asked David. "After all, we wasted so much time arguing with that forgetful old fraud back there."

"I'm sure. And he's not a fraud. Look what he can do: change signs and take white pigeons from his hat. Why, I've never even seen a white pigeon before. All the pigeons in New York are a kind of filthy gray. Anyone who can do that *must* be magic."

They turned to the right at the signs and walked quite a way before they finally found themselves at a door that opened onto a ledge above the subway rails. They had to walk about fifty steps before they came at last to the crowded station.

"Isn't that funny," said Leilah. "I've always noticed these strange doors in the subway tunnel when I rode on the trains. But it never occurred to me that they might be connected to a wizard's walkway."

David didn't answer. Instead he kept glancing nervously down the track, trying to see whether a subway train was coming. He stood first on one leg and then on the other. He didn't want to admit to Leilah that he was scared. After all, he had never ridden on a subway before. And Leilah was as calm as could be. But David had to admit to himself that he *was* uneasy as he heard a faint rumbling in the distance. He glanced down the track again.

"Not that way, silly. It's coming from the other way," said Leilah.

David felt so stupid that he forgot his fears as the subway train drew closer. It did not even bother him that the crowd behind them began to push them toward the tracks. Suddenly the entire station seemed to shake as the red and green lights on the first car came hurtling down the track into the station. The train filled the entire subway stop with its screeching, rocking, rattling presence. Before he could think, David had been pushed through the wide-open doors, against people fighting to get out, and on into the train. He looked around frantically and saw Leilah wiggle through a small opening between an enormous lady carrying two brown shopping bags, and a man with a drooping moustache, carrying a black leather portfolio.

"I'll show you where we get off," Leilah shouted above the din of the train. But it was too noisy to hear anything, so they rode to Fifty-ninth Street without talking further.

Leilah had to drag David off when they reached their stop. He had become mesmerized by the constant shaking and banging of the train and might have ridden all day if she hadn't grabbed his hand. She pulled him up the stairs and pointed them both in the right direction. David was delighted to see daylight again.

They took off down the avenue at a gallop, kicking their heels like ponies let out to pasture, barely missing a little old lady with an umbrella she was using against the sun and a beggar who wore a sign proclaiming that he was blind though he stepped quickly and expertly out of their way, lifting his dark glasses to watch them as they passed.

As they came to Fifty-eighth Street, Leilah pointed across the street. In the middle of the block they saw the same sign they had seen in the tapestry: *J. Pickwell. VIP Interiors.*

David and Leilah crossed over without paying any attention to the light. Luckily it was green.

"Look," said Leilah.

David looked. There in the window, standing rigidly on the top of a graceful Hepplewhite table, was the marble statue of D. Dog. And Mr. Pickwell was reaching over to pick it up and show it to a customer.

A Priceless Possession

This statue is priceless," Mr. Pickwell was saying to a woman in a mink coat and her husband as David and Leilah burst into his store.

"Nonsense," said the lady. "The price is right on it. Two hundred dollars."

"Rather than priceless, I'd call it overpriced," her husband added.

"Overpriced!" said Pickwell, his Adam's apple bobbing indignantly. "For a genuine sixteenth-century Italian marble statue? Over four hundred years old? Why, at that price it's a steal!"

"It sure is," shouted David breathlessly. "And you stole it from me. That's my dog. And he isn't any four hundred years old. He's seven and a half. And here is the twenty dollars you gave me for him."

With that, David grabbed D. Dog, threw the money down on the table, and raced out. Leilah was right behind him.

"Stop, you little thief!" cried Pickwell. "Come back!"

If David and Leilah heard him, they gave no sign, but ran down the block without looking right or left, straight into a great big blue stomach that was attached to a six-foot-three policeman.

"Now hold on there, youngsters," said the policeman. "And where are you going in such a hurry?"

Just then Pickwell came out of his store, shouting. When he saw the patrolman with David and Leilah, he ran over and grabbed the statue from David's hands. "Thank goodness you caught them, Sergeant. They were trying to steal this from my store."

"Is that true?" the policeman asked the children, but gently, for he had a son and daughter just their age at home.

"It's my dog," said David tearfully. "He stole it from me first. I was just stealing it back."

"The boy must have this dog confused with some other," said Pickwell smoothly. "I'm Joseph Pickwell of VIP Interiors," he said, and insinuated his calling card into the policeman's hand. "Why, this statue is one of my most priceless possessions. I even display it in my shop with some trepidation. What on earth would a boy like this be doing with a sixteenth-century dog by Bonetelli, the famous Florentine sculptor?" When he said "Bonetelli," Mr. Pickwell's eyeglasses popped from his nose and his waxed moustache quivered.

"That's not Bonetelli's dog. That's mine," said David. "At least it was until the Wizard changed it into a statue this morning. And he can't change it back unless I bring it to his warren." When he saw the policeman looking bewildered, he added, "It's the touching that counts."

The policeman smiled sympathetically at David while he patted him on the head, and winked at Mr. Pickwell. Then he took David and Leilah by the hand. "Now you two children had better go home. And don't let me catch you around here again. If I do, I'm afraid I'll have to take you to juvenile court. And I really wouldn't like to do that."

"Thank you, *Sergeant,*" said Mr. Pickwell, though he knew very well the policeman was only a patrolman. "I can see you are a man of discretion and understanding." And with a tight little smile, he adjusted his eyeglasses on his nose again and hurried back into his shop.

"But, officer," David began. "It really *is* my dog, and—"

"I'll take him home, sir. And thanks for letting us go," said Leilah, pulling David toward the subway.

The policeman watched until they started down the subway stairs then went to his call box and complained that nothing interesting ever happened on his beat.

As they went down the stairs David said, "You're a traitor, Leilah. Why didn't you back me up? You know it's true."

"Of course it's true," said Leilah. "But you'll never convince an adult of it. Especially a policeman. They have no imagination, adults. They don't believe in magic. The only thing left to do is go back to the Wizard and see if he can help."

"Oh, great," said David. "Some help he's been so far. If it hadn't been for his help in the first place, we wouldn't need his help in the second place."

"Well, smarty, any other ideas?" asked Leilah.

"None," said David glumly, reaching into his pocket for his lunch dollar to pay the subway fare. "Hey, it's gone!"

"What's gone?" asked Leilah.

"My dollar. I must have given it to old Pickleface with the other money. We'll have to go back and get it, otherwise how can I get into the subway?"

"Well, we can't go back, because we'll be arrested by the policeman," said Leilah sensibly. "We'll just have to walk."

"Walk?" said David. "How far is it?"

"Well, since we're on Fifty-ninth Street and Lexington Avenue, it's fifty-nine blocks and two avenues."

"That'll take hours," said David.

"Let's see . . . if twenty blocks make a mile, that's about three miles," said Leilah. "If we could walk a mile in twenty minutes, twenty blocks in twenty minutes . . . we'd have to walk a block a minute. And if the lights are with us and not too many people slow us down, we could be back at the Square in about an hour."

They started off at a brisk pace, walking a block a minute by David's watch. They had to pause at several red lights, losing five minutes in all and causing David to shift from one leg to another and snap his fingers nervously each time they waited. But in less than an hour, because Leilah had forgotten that Washington Square is on Sixth Street and not on First Street at all, and because in the end they decided to run one block and walk the next, the Arch loomed ahead of them.

"We're here!" shouted David, who was beginning to limp because the heel of his sock had slipped down into his shoe and had rubbed a blister. He began to run toward the Arch, favoring the one foot.

Leilah started to run with him, but stopped abruptly and shouted, "David—look!"

David stopped and followed her finger. There, under the Arch, was the Wizard. His pointed cap was quivering. And he was shaking hands with a tall, skinny man with a waxed moustache.

"It's old Pickleface Pickwell," said David. "What's he doing here? And why is he shaking hands with *our* Wizard?"

As they watched, Pickwell got into a large truck that was standing by. It said *Pickwell Pick-up* on the side. Then he drove off. The Wizard, his hands clasped behind him and his head down, walked back into the Arch.

"They must have been in cahoots all along," said David. "Why, I bet that old Wizard goes around turning dogs and cats (and maybe even people) into statues and then Pickwell sells them as 'priceless possessions.' "

"David, what a gruesome thing to say," Leilah protested. But her protest sounded faint, even in her own ears.

David went on. "Think of all the animals and people that are missing every year. I bet they are all on display in someone's living room."

Leilah looked thoughtful. "I had an Uncle William John who went out for groceries one day and never returned. We suspected he ran off to Tahiti."

"Your Uncle William John is probably standing marble-fied in some rich person's garden, snowed on in winter, rained on in spring, leafed on in the fall, and carrying a summer bird's nest in his hair."

"Poor Uncle Billy Jack," said Leilah sadly. Then she giggled. "And he never could stand birds, either."

"It's not funny," said David. But they both started giggling uncontrollably at the thought of Leilah's Uncle William John with robins nesting in his Italian marble hair.

"But if it's true," said Leilah suddenly, "then the Wizard is a menace. Maybe we ought to call the police."

David shook his head. "Leilah, you said yourself that no adults would believe us. We'll have to do it ourselves. We'll have to face him in his warren." He stood up as tall as he could. "We owe D. Dog that much."

"But I don't want to end up a statue too," wailed Leilah.

David didn't either. But once he had made up his mind, he rarely changed it. And so he said, more bravely than he really felt, "Nothing will happen. We'll tell him we've sent letters home to our parents to be opened in case we disappear. And they will know who is to blame and go directly to the police if anything happens to us."

"But that's not true. No one will know *anything* if we disappear," said Leilah.

"You know that and I know that," said David. "But the Wizard doesn't."

It seemed like a good plan on first thought. So without waiting to give it a second thought, David and Leilah opened the door to the Arch and went down the twisting tunnel toward the Wizard's warren. They were really frightened, though neither would admit it. But when they reached the door to the warren, Leilah's hands were shaking uncontrollably and David's teeth were chattering a complicated rhythm. However, drawing in deep breaths at the same time, they pulled the door open and bravely walked in.

THE TABLE'S PART

The Wizard was seated in the chair that controlled the tapestry. He was concentrating on a scene. By the time they got to the tapestry, David and Leilah could see the picture clearly. It was Mr. Pickwell and he was arranging the statue of D. Dog on a new table.

"But that table—it . . . it's . . ." began David.

The Wizard sighed. "It's *my* table, all right. And I hope it's in a good mood. If it does anything foolish, we're all sunk." And he took his pointed hat off and ran his fingers through his long white hair.

"But why does Old Pickleface have your table?" asked David.

The Wizard looked pleased. "I was hoping you'd ask that," he said. "It's part of my plan."

"What plan?" asked David and Leilah fearfully.

"Why, my plan to rescue the statue, bring it here, and try to turn it back into a real live dog again."

"You mean," said David, smiling, "that you aren't in cahoots with Pickwell? That you don't turn animals into statues for a living and then sell them to rich people to keep in their gardens?"

"My dear child, whatever are you talking about?" asked the Wizard. He looked so genuinely puzzled that David and Leilah realized how foolish their thoughts had been.

"Never mind," said Leilah. "Just tell us your plan."

"Well," the Wizard began, running his fingers through his beard and freeing a butterfly that had become entangled there, "I saw what happened to you through the tapestry. And when I realized how long it would take you to walk home, I knew I had to do what I could on my own. But I also knew that I didn't dare trust the magic. So I telephoned Mr. Pickwell from the pay phone in the park and said I was interested in selling my table to him if he was still interested in buying it. He harumphed a bit, but when I said *cheap* he agreed to my one stipulation. That was that he himself come down immediately and pick it up. That way, you see, I knew he would be out of his store and so could not sell the statue before my plan went into action. The only difficult thing was to persuade the table to go along with the whole scheme. But I managed to get its ball away from it, and so it was forced to agree. Of course, it kicked me once during the scramble." The Wizard paused to lift his robe up until his knee was showing. He had an enormous black-and-blue-and-green-and-yellow mark on his shin. "But if my plan works, it was worth it."

"What is your plan?" asked David.

At that moment, Leilah, who had been watching the tapestry out of the corner of her eye, cried, "Look!"

David and Leilah moved closer to the tapestry. They saw Pickwell talking to a customer in his store, his back to the table. The table was calmly scratching its drawer handle with a front leg.

"Oh, you promised . . ." said the Wizard.

David and Leilah and the Wizard looked away, counted to sixty, then looked back again at the new picture framed by the floral border. All in all, they watched almost an hour until the drama was played out.

Pickwell was haggling with a customer on the price of one of his "priceless possessions"—an unbreakable lamp base made from the tusks of a rogue elephant. Indian, of course. They settled at last upon $72.97, when a rattling made them turn around. The table had shifted its weight to a back leg, and the statue of D. Dog had slipped a little to the right.

("Oh, no!" David and Leilah said together. The Wizard just gasped.)

Mr. Pickwell came over to investigate, decided it was mice, and made a notation on his cuff to call the exterminator in the morning. Then he stepped into the back of his shop to wrap the unbreakable Indian elephant-tusk lamp base. Meanwhile the customer went down into the basement to look at *Pickwell's Pick-overs* (*Nothing higher than fifty dollars*), the VIP bargains. The minute Pickwell left the room, the table stepped gingerly out of the window, balancing carefully so that the statue of D. Dog did not slip off. Then, with a quick two-step, the table walked past some large Victorian chairs and a grape-pattern stuffed sofa, patted a dainty schoolmarm desk on the drawer with one leg, and headed for the door. The table pushed the door open and sidled out silently just as Mr. Pickwell emerged from the back with a large brown paper package tied with a bright red string. The door slammed shut and Pickwell, thinking it was a customer leaving, ran over to the door. He leaned out and saw the table calmly walking down the street.

("Run!" shouted David at this point. To the table, of course, not to Pickwell. But of course the table could not hear him.)

Pickwell was so surprised that he dropped the lamp, which broke into several large pieces. Stepping over the pieces, Pickwell started shouting, "Stop, table, stop, thief. Someone stop that table."

Several people turned to look at him, but since everyone knew that tables couldn't really walk, they chuckled and guessed it was just an advertising stunt and did not try to help.

The policeman, the same one who had stopped David and Leilah before, heard the shouts and came running. When he finally understood that Pickwell wanted him to chase and arrest a runaway table, he threatened to take him in for disturbing the peace and possible drunk-and-disorderly. He knew as well as anyone that tables can't walk.

And through all this fuss, the Wizard's table calmly walked to the IRT, took a token from its center drawer, and went over the turnstile carefully so as not to break the statue.

The subways going downtown were not crowded and no

one was pushed by the table. Consequently, no one noticed it either. As soon as the subway reached Cooper Square, the table got off and went through the door into the tunnel. The children and the Wizard came out to the fork in the tunnel to greet it. David grabbed the statue of D. Dog and hugged it tightly.

Leilah took one of the table's legs in her hand and shook it enthusiastically.

And the Wizard was so pleased with himself, he did a little dance all the way back through the twisting tunnel to the warren.

Once in his room, the Wizard brought out a golden flask. "This calls for a celebration," he said. He poured a little of the liquid into goblets for David and Leilah and himself. And he even poured a little on the table top. David and Leilah watched as the liquid was absorbed. It was an amber-colored drink, yet it also reflected the light in rainbow colors, and beautiful shadows seemed to suggest themselves in the goblets.

"It's delicious," said Leilah at her first sip. "What is it?"

"Nectar," said the Wizard. "The drink of the old gods."

They finished their nectar in silence, each thinking god-like thoughts.

Finally David said, "Now all we have to do is turn the statue back into a real live dog and—" he was stroking the statue as he spoke and he suddenly stopped. "It's chipped! The statue is chipped. Here, look. On the back leg. There's a piece missing."

"Oh my," said the Wizard. "So there is." He shook his fist

at the table. "See what you did. You weren't careful enough. Making eyes at that schoolmarm desk instead of tending to your own business. I ought to turn you into firewood!"

"It's just a *little* chip," soothed Leilah. "Will it make a difference?"

"I don't know," said the Wizard. "I don't know. It might spoil the spell. It's been known to happen. Pieces of things getting stuck in the works and all that. All we can do is go ahead and hope."

"Okay," said David. "What do we do?"

"First, I think we should all go out where it all began. With the swinging statues, I mean. I'm sure if anything is going to happen, it will happen there."

Leilah collected the goblets and put them gently in the large wooden wine vat the Wizard seemed to use as a sink. The Wizard put the golden nectar bottle back on the shelf amid dozens of other colorful bottles. Then David, with the statue in his hands, led the way up the twisting tunnel.

They pushed open the door to the park and the sunlight blinded them momentarily, so they didn't see the owner of the voice that shouted, "Stop, thieves. Come back with my table and my statue."

But they didn't need to see to know who it was—Mr. Joseph Pickwell himself, stepping out of a taxi. He had guessed that the table would return to its original owner, and as soon as the policeman had let him go, he grabbed a taxi and hurried downtown once more.

"What do we do now?" wailed Leilah.

"I don't know," said the Wizard.

David started to shut the door.

At that moment Pickwell, umbrella in hand, reached the Arch and pushed open the door.

"Got you," he cried as he grabbed for the statue in David's hand.

THE CHASE

L eilah screamed.

David slammed the door in Pickwell's face and leaned his back against it. But he was too light to hold the door shut and it began to move open slowly as Pickwell pushed. Leilah and the Wizard rushed to help David.

"How long can you two keep it shut by yourselves?" asked the Wizard.

"Not much more than a minute," said David.

"Well, give me the statue," said the Wizard. "I'll take it back to the warren and see if I can conjure up something. You hold Mr. Pickwell off as long as you can." He took the statue and scurried away in the darkness as fast as an old mole in its tunnel.

David and Leilah struggled with the door but it kept inching inward. They could hear Pickwell's heavy breathing on the other side and an occasional murmur. "Thieves. Ingrates. Beatniks."

"Tell you what," David whispered to Leilah. "When I say three, we'll jump aside. Maybe he'll be leaning so hard, he'll fall on his face. At least that's what always happens in the movies. Then we'll run ahead and try to trip him up at the fork. Don't forget the first time we came how we felt off balance in the tunnel. Well, Pickleface will probably feel that way, too."

"All right," Leilah whispered back. "I'm ready when you say so."

David took a deep breath. "Here goes," he said. "One . . . two . . . three!"

They jumped back and started to run. From the noise and grunts and mutters they heard as they raced away, David had guessed right. Pickwell had been pushing so hard that when the door opened suddenly, he had been caught off guard and had fallen through. Trying to break his fall with his umbrella, Pickwell fell on the handle and broke it instead, knocking himself out of breath. It was just enough time to give David and Leilah a good head start down the tunnel.

They arrived quite quickly at the fork and started down the path toward the warren.

"Wait a minute," said Leilah. "We'll lead him right to the statue and the table this way. Let's switch signs so that he won't think of going to the warren at all." And with that, she reached up on tiptoe to try to take the sign down. She was scarcely an inch too short. But she couldn't reach the sign. Then David tried. But he and Leilah were the same height.

"I'll give you a boost up," said David. "But hurry."

He knelt on all fours, and Leilah clambered up on his

back. Teetering slightly, she took down the WARREN sign. Then they brought it over to the right-hand branch. David knelt down again and Leilah scrambled up on his back. She exchanged the DRAGONRY sign for the WARREN sign. Then they hurried back to the place where the WARREN sign used to be and hung the sign DRAGONRY in its place. Just as Leilah was climbing down, they heard Pickwell's labored breathing coming down the tunnel.

"There," Leilah whispered to David with satisfaction, "no one in his right mind would go to a dragonry."

"Well, maybe he's not in his right mind," said David. "Or maybe he can't read."

"We'll soon find out," said Leilah grimly.

The children drew back into the tunnel that led to the warren and hugged the damp, mossy wall. They were well into the shadows and could not be seen.

"If worse comes to worst," David said, "we can still try to trip him."

Under the far lantern light they could see Pickwell making his slow way toward them.

"Shh, don't make a sound," said David.

"I'm too scared to," Leilah whispered back.

At last Pickwell came to the fork. He glanced at the signs and dismissed DRAGONRY and IRT with quick snorts. He turned down the tunnel marked WARREN.

"It worked!" Leilah whispered when Pickwell had disappeared. "He's headed for the dragonry."

David clapped her on the back. "That was brilliant!"

Just then they heard a small splash followed by a loud

yelp. David grabbed Leilah's hand. "Let's go and see what's happening," he said.

"Happening?" said Leilah, pulling away. "What's happening is that we're getting out of here."

But David had tiptoed down the tunnel. When Leilah got to him, he was standing with his hand over his mouth.

"It was big and white and had teeth," he said. "I think . . . I think it was an alligator. It took Old Pickleface by the seat of his pants and crawled into the water. He was waving his umbrella about and sputtering. Pickwell, I mean. Not the alligator."

Leilah nodded. She had heard about the big white alligators that were supposed to live in the sewers below New York. Once they had been baby alligators sent as presents to the city's children from grandparents and rich uncles who lived in Florida. But the mothers had flushed them—the alligators, not the rich uncles—down the toilets. And so the alligators grew and flourished in the dark world beneath the streets, growing fat on sewer rats and white in the always-dark world.

"Maybe we should rescue him?" Leilah asked tentatively.

"Are you crazy?" asked David, and for a moment he really believed she was. "Then they'll get us too. The alligators."

"But we can't just let him . . . die or something," Leilah protested.

"Why not?" David said bitterly. "Look what he was going to do with D. Dog. And the table. And us."

"Well, that is hardly cause to let him die," said Leilah. "I think we'd better go and find out whether the Wizard can help." It wasn't a statement. It was a command.

"Nonsense," said the Wizard after he heard about Mr. Pickwell's predicament. "The alligators won't eat him. They may be only alligators, but they *do* have taste."

And so it was, some two hours later, that Mr. Pickwell climbed out of a manhole cover on Forty-second Street and Broadway. He was soaking wet, scratched, and fuming. His temper was as foul as his clothes, for he had traveled the length and breadth of the New York sewers in the alligator's mouth. And when a policeman arrested him for, of all things, obstructing traffic, Mr. Pickwell tried to hit the officer with his now broken umbrella. It was another hour before Mr. Pickwell's papers had dried out enough so that he could prove to the police sergeant at the station house that he was a Very Important Personage. By then, his moustache was completely unwaxed and wiltted, and he looked very little like the picture in his wallet. He finally phoned his lawyer, who paid his bond and got him out of jail for the night, though he would still have to return to stand trial for assaulting a police officer. Mr. Joseph Pickwell of VIP Interiors went home in a twit.

"Poor man," said Leilah, clucking sympathetically, for they had watched it all in the tapestry. But David and the Wizard were chuckling.

"I always thought he was all wet!" said the Wizard happily.

RECALLED

It was just barely nine o'clock when David and Leilah met at the base of the Arch on Monday morning. David had almost beaten the sun up. He had surprised his mother and father at the breakfast table with the announcement that he had found a friend—indeed, several friends (for he counted the table, too)—and would be at the park all day again. His mother wondered whether he oughtn't bring the friends around so they could see them. But David's father was so pleased that he shushed David's mother immediately and gave David two dollars for lunch and a treat for his friends.

The Wizard was ten minutes late and still yawning when he appeared at the door with the statue. It had remained in the warren for safekeeping. No one had worried about Pickwell showing up, but to be sure, they had switched the signs back. The Wizard guessed—correctly, as it turned out—that Pickwell would not come to the Village again. He had had enough.

"Sorry to be late," the Wizard said. "But I was up past

midnight studying some spells that might help us, and I overslept this morning."

"Did you find anything?" asked Leilah.

"I'm not sure," said the Wizard. "I wrote them down, though, and put them under my hat."

"Oh, great," said David. "We might find them next week sometime."

"No, no, child," said the Wizard. "Not that hat. My nightcap."

"And when does it give back things?" asked David. "On the full moon?"

"The next morning. Always!" said the Wizard as he brought out his nightcap from a pocket in his robe. He reached into the cap and extracted a small scrap of lined paper on which was written a short couplet. "We'll have to play the game, though. Just like the last time." He smiled. "At least if this doesn't work, we'll have some fun."

"But what if you change David and me into statues by mistake?" said Leilah.

"There's that, of course," said the Wizard.

"Yes," David pointed out sarcastically. "It's the touching, you know."

"That's true," said the Wizard, admiration in his voice. "However did you know? That's a wizard's secret."

"You said it often enough," said David.

"Oh, I shouldn't have. I couldn't have. I'm not supposed to. I must have forgotten," said the Wizard, looking around over his shoulder as though someone might be watching. "But it's true, you know," he whispered confidentially.

"About the touching, I mean. So I had already decided not to swing you two but to concentrate on the statue."

They walked over to the grassy area and took their places. David and Leilah pretended that they had just been swung around and made statues. David stood like a sword swallower swallowing the world's longest sword. Leilah was a snake that had just dined on a pink hippocampus.

The Wizard stood between them and started to swing around, holding the marble statue in one arm and the piece of paper in the other. He squinted at the verse he had written and chanted:

> "Swinging here, swinging there,
> Swinging statues everywhere,
> Sage and parsley, thyme and chive,
> Help me bring 'em back alive."

When he had finished the verse, he threw the statue into the air. It went straight up and started down, turning end over end over end.

"Hey," shouted David, "wait a minute! You'll break it! It's already chipped." He ran under the falling statue and waited for it to come down. He spread his arms to catch it and missed. David closed his eyes, expecting to hear it shatter on the ground. But what he heard was D. Dog barking and whining, and when he opened his eyes he saw his terrier jumping up and wriggling and doing all the dog things he had been saving to do for a day.

"You did it! You did it!" squealed Leilah. "That was first-class magic, even if you did have to peek at your paper."

But the Wizard did not hear her. He was still whirling around and around. A curious humming sound was in the air, and under the Wizard a small whirlwind was building up. First it picked up pieces of dust and dirt and old candy wrappers. Then it gathered in half-eaten peanuts and peanut shells, back pages of the *Village Voice* and the jacket of a Grove Press novel. And at last it picked up the Wizard himself. As he began to rise in the air, the wind blew his beard straight up as if pointing the way. His eyes were closed and his face had an ecstatic smile.

"Where are you going?" shouted David above the humming. "Wait—we haven't thanked you yet. I even have money for a special treat. Wait. . . ."

Just as he cleared the tops of the maples, the Wizard looked down at David and Leilah and at a small crowd of bearded young men and long-haired young women who had gathered there. "Recalled. Recalled," he shouted down happily. "I'm going home. Recalled."

"Will you ever come back?" Leilah yelled up as loudly as she could, afraid that he could not hear her in the rush of wind.

"If you need me, I will come. We are bound by the Rule of Need," came a voice out of the whirlwind. "Recalled. . . ."

Like a gas-filled balloon that has escaped from a child's fingers, the Wizard rose slowly at first, then faster and faster, a small speck in the sky rising higher and higher until at last he disappeared.

"That sure is some trip," said one of the bearded young men. They laughed and went on their way with the long-haired women.

David and Leilah looked until they could see nothing more. Then they waited silently a few minutes longer to be sure.

"Is he gone? Really gone?" asked Leilah, afraid she might have to cry.

"I guess so," said David who was hugging D. Dog and starting to sniffle—just a little—himself.

"What about all his stuff in the warren?" asked Leilah.

"Are you kidding?" David said. "After that whirlwind, moving furniture should be a breeze!"

Leilah giggled. "That's a pretty good joke!" she said.

They walked out of the park, D. Dog at their heels, and started toward an ice-cream man who was coming down Fifth Avenue.

"Do you believe it *really* happened?" asked David. "I mean—really?"

"Look at D. Dog," said Leilah, pointing at the terrier, who was running ahead of them now.

"What do you mean?" asked David as he looked. D. Dog turned and started to run back toward them. He was limping slightly on his right rear paw.

"The chipped foot," said David.

"Exactly," said Leilah.

"Well, will we ever see the Wizard again?" David asked.

"I guess so. If we *really* need him," Leilah answered.

"What I *really* need now is an ice cream," said David. "My treat!"

And smiling secret smiles, the two friends ran up to the vendor to get their cones.

ABOUT THE AUTHOR

JANE YOLEN is the distinguished author of more than 250 books for children, teens, and adults. She has earned many awards over the years, including the World Fantasy Award, two Nebula Awards, the Society of Children's Book Writers Golden Kite Award, three Mythopoeic Society Asian Award, two Christopher Medals, the Boy's Club Jr. Book Award, the Garden State Teen Book Award, the California Young Reader's Medal, New York State's Charlotte Award, the Daedalus Award, a number of Parents' Choice Awards, four Honorary Doctorates, and many more awards and citations for her work.

Ms. Yolen lives in with her husband in Hatfield, Massachusetts, and St. Andrews, Scotland.

Look for

paythepiper

by Jane Yolen AND Adam Stemple

Available July 2005
From Tom Doherty Associates